TALES

THE BOY WHO CRIED HORSE

by Terry Deary

illustrated by Helen Flook

PiCTURE WiNDOW BOOKS
Minneapolis, Minnesota

Editor: Shelly Lyons
Page Production: Michelle Biedscheid
Art Director: Nathan Gassman
Associate Managing Editor: Christianne Jones

First American edition published in 2008 by
Picture Window Books
5115 Excelsior Boulevard
Suite 232
Minneapolis, MN 55416
877-845-8392
www.picturewindowbooks.com

First published in 2007 by A&C Black Publishers Limited, 38 Soho Square,
London W1D 3HB, with the title THE BOY WHO CRIED HORSE.

Printed in the United States of America.

 All books published by Picture Window Books
are manufactured with paper containing at least
10 percent post-consumer waste.

Library of Congress Cataloging-in-Publication Data
Deary, Terry.
The boy who cried horse / by Terry Deary ; illustrated by Helen
Flook — 1st American ed.
p. cm. — (Read-it! chapter books) (Historical tales)
Summary: In Troy in 1180 B.C., Acheron, storyteller in the palace of
Paris and Helen, is so well-known as a liar that when a wooden horse
left by the enemy Greek army rouses his suspicion and he learns truth
about the deadly threat it holds, no one will believe him. Includes
facts about Troy and its destruction.
ISBN-13: 978-1-4048-4049-2 (library binding)
[1. Honesty—Fiction. 2. Trojan War—Fiction. 3. Paris (Legendary
character)—Fiction. 4. Helen of Troy (Greek mythology)—Fiction.
5. Mythology, Greek—Fiction. 6. Troy (Extinct city)—Fiction.] I. Flook,
Helen, ill. II. Title.
PZ7.D3517Boy 2008
[Fic]—dc22   2007035611

Table of Contents

Words to Know

Achilles—an ancient Greek hero of the Trojan War; it is said that he was killed in battle when an arrow pierced his heel

Aesop—a Greek storyteller whose fables teach a lesson

lyre—a stringed instrument that was played by ancient Greeks

Trojan—relating to ancient Troy

Troy—a city featured in the *Iliad*, a long poem written by a storyteller named Homer

Chapter One

The Finest City

Troy, 1180 B.C.

Aesop the Greek storyteller said:
There is no believing a liar, even
when he speaks the truth.

My name is Acheron. I live in the ruined city of Troy. It once was the finest city in the world. But now, it's gone. The wind blows across the plains and covers the stone ruins with sand and dust.

How can this be? How could a mighty city turn into a crumbling ruin in my lifetime?

I will tell you, if you will listen. Troy would still be there now, if they had listened to me back then. The trouble was, I told lies. But I'm not lying now.

You believe me, don't you? I am Acheron the Liar—the last Trojan. And this is my story.

Chapter Two

The Lying Poet

My mother used to tell me stories.

"I'll never forget the day you were born," she'd say. "Prince Paris came to Troy that day. He stood upon the palace steps and spoke to us all."

Then, Mother would stand and raise her chin. Her eyes would gaze into the distance, and she became our prince. "People Trojan, greet you I with deep joy, godly thanks give us for journey safely homeward be today in shiply sail," she would say.

"Why does he speak like that?" I
would ask.

"Our Paris is good with a sword but
hopeless with words," she would say.

Then she'd tell me how Paris showed the Trojans his new wife, Queen Helen. "She was lovelier than a great steak pie," Mother sighed.

You see, we were starving every day, and *nothing* was lovelier than a great steak pie. We were lucky to get a little rat meat in our watery soup.

The trouble was, Prince Paris had stolen Queen Helen from the Greeks. And shortly after Paris arrived back in Troy, the Greeks came looking for her.

"We want her back!" her husband, Menelaus, said. "We'll stay right here, outside your walls, until you all starve to death."

"Not a chancely hopeful thing, think I," Prince Paris said as he laughed. "We overstuffy with foodlets!"

In the palace, Prince Paris found ways
to feed the people. Troy was a huge city
with many little gates to sneak food
through. There was a deep well in the
marketplace, so we had plenty of water.

The best food in Troy always went to Paris and Helen. The second-best food went to the fighting soldiers who stood guard on Troy's massive outer walls. It also went to the many people working in the palace.

The rest of us were left to live on scraps or any rats we could catch.

But soon even the rats were as thin as the east wind that blew across the plains of Troy.

I decided to become a storyteller at the palace, so I could eat pie.

Every Friday, Paris and Helen had a feast at the palace. They ate huge pies filled with tender goat meat and topped with thick gravy. The poets sang stories about the Trojan heroes and were paid with a pie.

I learned to write poems, and I sang them to Paris and Helen. The poems were usually so long that they lasted for half of a feast.

Of course, the tales I told were lies. I made Paris and the Trojan heroes sound like gods, because that's what Paris and Helen wanted to hear. I made the Greeks appear as weak as the seaweed that had washed up on the shores where their ships rested.

So, you see, I was a liar. If you were hungry, then you would have lied, too.

Chapter Three

The Mysterious Stranger

On the last Friday evening most Trojans
would ever see,
I met a stranger
on the road
to the palace.
He was an old
man with a
gray beard and
a dusty robe.
He slipped
out from the
shadow of a
side street and
stopped me.

He pointed at the tortoise shell I was carrying. "You have a lyre," he said. "You must be a poet."

"I am," I answered. "I'm going to sing for Paris and Helen at the palace."

"Then I'll come along with you," he said. "You can show me the way."

"Everyone knows where the palace is," I said.

"I am a stranger to Troy," he told me.

I walked a few paces on the paved road and then stopped. "There are no strangers in Troy," I said. "The city has been locked for 10 years to keep out the Greeks. How did you get in?"

"There are ways," he said softly. "Lead on. Perhaps you can help me get inside the palace. I need to speak to Prince Paris."

"Why should I help you?" I asked.

"I'll give you all of the food you have ever dreamed of," he promised.

I said I'd lie to help him. If you were hungry, then you would have lied, too. I didn't know I would end up betraying my city.

We walked through the moonlit streets to the palace. The strong wind from the plains pushed us up the hill.

Soon, we reached the palace. The guards there knew me well and let me through. "Who's this?" they asked as they pointed at the man.

"My father," I lied. Truthfully, my father had died while fighting during the first weeks of the war. I had never known him. I always thought he would have been like this kind-eyed man.

The guards let the stranger pass. Inside, the palace hall was bustling with servants and guards, magicians and jugglers, dancers and musicians. I knew them all.

Torches flamed and crackled along the walls. A trumpet blasted out a horrible, tuneless fanfare.

"Ooops! Sorry, there were a few wrong notes in there!" the trumpeter said as his cheeks blushed. "I proudly present Prince Paris and Lady Helen!"

The people clapped politely as Paris entered. He was followed by Helen, the sour-mouthed Queen (that's what my mother called her).

Paris raised a hand and exclaimed, "Commencify us the juggly and the musi-magic songerly entertainables!"

The stranger muttered in my ear, "What is he saying?"

"I don't know," I said and shrugged. "It's all Greek to me."

We watched dancers snake and sway. A magician made a duck appear from a hat.

Then, it was my turn to perform. I stepped forward with my lyre in hand.

Just then, the stranger pushed me aside. He bowed before Paris.

"Whattalie wantable?" Paris asked.

"News," the stranger said. "I bring great news!"

Chapter Four

A Wooden Horse

"My name is Sinon, and I come from
the Greek camp," the stranger said.

Helen jumped to her feet and yelled,
"A *Greek* in Troy? Kill him! Kill him!"

There was a swish of swords as the guards marched forward.

Sinon raised a hand. "I hate the Greeks!" he cried. "They are cowards. Mighty Prince Paris here is greater than 10 Greek warriors!"

"It's truthly rightable," Paris said.

Sinon continued, "What I came to tell you is that the Greeks are running away from your city."

"Away?" Helen asked. Her sly eyes squinted at the old man.

"Back to Greece," said Sinon. "They say they have been here too long. They say they have more important things to do. They have sailed off in their ships and have left behind a mighty wooden statue to honor their heroes!"

"They *have* no heroes," Helen replied as she sneered.

"Their statue will stand on the windy plain of Troy for all the world to see," Sinon said softly. "Every ship that passes will see it and remember the Greek heroes."

"Statue?" Helen asked. "What is this statue? A statue of Achilles?"

"Paris princelet arrowed Achilleres in the heel-o and deaded him dead with tippy point poison!" Paris cried.

We all knew that story. Paris had been afraid to face the heroic Greek Achilles in battle, so he shot Achilles from behind with a poison arrow. Of course, I hadn't sung about *that*!

"It is the statue of a horse," Sinon continued. "You can see it from the city walls. Maybe it is a gift from the Greeks to noble Paris. It will stand there and remind you of them every day."

"No, it won't!" Helen roared.
"It won't?" Sinon asked.

"We will bring it into the city and use it for firewood. We will not let any passing ships see anything Greek," she raged. "Paris, give the order!"

"Ahem!" Paris cleared his throat. "Statute horsling insideify Troylum to getter sunshiny day."

The guards stood still. "What did he say?" they asked.

Helen explained, "Tomorrow at first light, we'll drag the wooden horse until it is inside the walls of this city."

"That will be hard work. We will need a lot of pies to give us strength," a guard grumbled.

"Now that the Greeks have gone, we'll never go hungry again. You will have pies tonight and pies every day of your life!" Helen promised.

Of course, she didn't know their "lives" from that night on would be short—very short.

Chapter Five

A Discovery

The feast began before I could sing my
new poem. I saw Sinon the stranger
slip out of the palace hall. I followed
him. I would return and sing for my pie
after the feast.

Sinon said he was a Greek who hated Greeks, but he didn't say why. I didn't trust him.

The stranger hurried back down the moonlit hill to the spot where he had met me. He turned into a dark alley and headed for the north wall of the city. I followed and watched.

A guard stood by the wall and waved a spear at Sinon. "Who goes there?" he demanded.

"Sinon the Greek-hater," the old man said. "You let me in, so now let me out."

"You promised me a pig's head if I let you in," the guard said.

"I'm off to get it," Sinon replied. "The Greeks left a lot of food behind."

The guard nodded. He pushed at a stone, and part of the wall slid open. Sinon patted his arm and walked out.

I ran to the gate.

"Acheron!" the guard cried.

"Shush, Cottus!" I hissed. "Let me out. I'm following that man."

"Don't you go eating any of the pigs those Greeks left behind. The first pig head is mine," he said.

"You already have a pig's head! It's on your own shoulders," I muttered, pushing my way through the opening in the wall.

Sinon was plodding over the plain. The Greek tents were gone, but broken swords and ashes from fires showed where they had been. I kept to the path around the edge of the plain and hid in the shadows of boulders.

We were close to the shore now, and
the moon was blocked by a huge shape.
There stood a wooden horse, almost as
tall as the walls of Troy.

Sinon waved to the horse as he walked
by it. At the water's edge, there was a
wooden pier that the Greeks had built.

A single ship stood waiting, and Sinon walked toward it. The wind carried the voices to me.

"Is it done, Sinon?" asked one voice.

"It is done," answered Sinon. "They take the horse in tomorrow morning."

"That's when we will return," said the other voice.

A rope was untied, and the ship was rowed out to sea.

It was a mystery. Sinon had said they were gone for good, so why were they talking of returning?

I wandered back toward Troy and looked up at the horse. On the moonlit side, I saw something I hadn't seen on my way out to the shore.

A rope ladder hung down the side of the horse. I heard voices of men, and the voices seemed to be coming from within the horse. I also heard the rattle of armor as the men moved around.

Then, I understood what was about to happen. I knew what I had to do.

I sped back to the wall of Troy. I called for Cottus to open the gate.

"Did you see that old feller with my pig's head?" he asked as the stone door swung open. "I want it on a plate."

"It will be *your* head on a plate tomorrow if you don't let me through! Quickly! I have to warn Prince Paris!"

I ran through the streets until my bare feet were stinging. I ran up the hill until my lungs were burning. Finally, I arrived at the palace, where I burst into the feast and cried, "Beware of the wooden horse!"

Chapter Six

A Truthful Song

"A singerly songerly!" Paris cried when
he saw me. The wine jugs were empty,
and the royal faces were as red as the
Trojan sunrise. Even the guards on
duty were drunk.

"The Greeks are planning a trick!" I cried.

"Singerly songerly!" Paris roared and banged the table with his knife handle.

"He wants you to give us one of your poems, Acheron," Helen cried.

I started to protest, "But—"

"Do it, or we will be eating *you* in a pie at the next feast," Helen snarled.

I had lost my lyre. I had no poem or song prepared. I had to make it up as I went along. I sang this warning:

The Greeks left a gift—a wooden horse. But it is not all it seems, you all know, of course!

The horse is stuffed with soldiers, fully armed. Once they are inside our walls, they will do us harm.

Just leave the horse out there upon the plain, or Troy will die and never rise again!

Helen picked up a knife and threw it at me. I ducked. It missed me and fell onto the marble floor. "That is the worst poem I've ever heard. You should die for that!" she exclaimed.

"But it's the truth!" I wailed.

"Acheron, you are a poet and a storyteller. It is your job to tell us lies! You tell us tales about how brave Paris is, and we all know that he really is a huge coward!" Helen screamed.

"Cowardy whobee? Songerlees of bravebold Paris trulyful is!" Paris tried to explain.

"You, Acheron, wouldn't know the truth if it jumped out of a pie and smacked you in the eye. You can't go making our feast gloomy with your tales of Greek victory," Helen hissed. She turned to the guards at the table and yelled, "Execute the liar!"

I turned and ran. I tumbled down
the hill to my home. Once I entered my
house, I shook my mother awake and
dragged her to the secret gate. We left
the city and walked out onto the plain.

We rested among the rocks that
night and slept among the sweet scent
of flowers. We would be free.

We awoke to the terrible sound of squealing wheels.

The wooden horse was about to be dragged through the great main gates of Troy.

Chapter Seven

Troy's Ending

You know the rest of the tale, I guess.
Once inside the city, the Greek soldiers
climbed out of the wooden horse and
opened the gates.

The Greek army returned, just as I had said they would.

They slaughtered every man and boy in Troy, including Paris. My mother and I were the exception. We were hiding in the hills.

Every woman and girl was carried off to be a slave to the Greeks. Helen was taken home to her husband.

The mighty city burned and fell.
The walls cracked and crumbled in the
heat. The city of Troy died that day.

My mother and I lived among the
ruins for many years.

That was a long time ago. Now there is only one Trojan left to tell the truth.

I'm sure the Greek poets sing their side of the story. I am left to sing mine alone. My song is called "The Boy Who Cried Horse."

The trouble was, I told lies. But I'm not lying now.

As Aesop the Greek storyteller said, "There is no believing a liar, even when he speaks the truth."

You believe me, don't you? I am Acheron the Liar—the last Trojan. And that was my story.

Afterword

The story of the wooden horse of Troy is one of the oldest stories in the world. We don't know if it is truth or legend. It is probably a bit of both.

The Greek army set off to attack Troy but couldn't break down the walls. They sat there for 10 years— some say from 1193 until 1183 B.C.

The ruins of Troy prove that the city was destroyed. But we may never know the cause of its destruction.

Five hundred years after the fall of Troy, a storyteller named Homer told the tale of Troy as a long poem. But we don't know if Homer's story is true.

Much later, a Roman writer named Virgil told us a bit more about the wooden horse in his own poem.

Was there really a spy named Sinon? Did this man sneak in and tell Paris to open the gates for the horse? Virgil said so. But Homer said Sinon spoke up after the horse was in the city.

Stories change over time, and the truth can be lost.

"The Boy Who Cried Horse" is based on Virgil's tale of Troy.

But is the tale of a hollow horse really true?

On the Web

FactHound offers a safe, fun way to find Web sites related to topics in this book. All of the sites on FactHound have been researched by our staff.

1. Visit *www.facthound.com*
2. Type in this special code:
   1404840494
3. Click on the FETCH IT button.

Your trusty FactHound will fetch the best sites for you!

Look for more *Read-It!* Reader Chapter Books: Historical Tales: